THE GIRL FROM THE GREAT SANDY DESERT

This is a Magabala Book

LEADING PUBLISHER OF ABORIGINAL AND
TORRES STRAIT ISLANDER STORYTELLERS.

CHANGING THE WORLD, ONE STORY AT A TIME.

First published 2015, reprinted 2019, 2020
New Edition 2024
Magabala Books Aboriginal Corporation
1 Bagot Street, Broome, Western Australia
Website: www.magabala.com Email: sales@magabala.com

Magabala Books is assisted by the Australian Government through Creative Australia, its principal arts investment and advisory body. The State of Western Australia has made an investment in this project through the Department of Local Government, Sport and Cultural Industries.

Magabala Books is an independent Aboriginal and Torres Strait Islander publishing house. We acknowledge the Traditional owners of the Country on which we live and work. We recognise and respect the unbroken connections to traditional lands, waters, and cultures. Through what we publish we honour all our Elders, peoples and stories, past, present and into our collective futures.

Cover Design Jo Hunt
Typeset by Post Pre-press Group
Printed and bound by Griffin Press, South Australia

978-1-922613-82-0 (Paperback)

A catalogue record for this book is available from the National Library of Australia

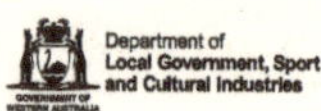

THE GIRL FROM THE GREAT SANDY DESERT

JUKUNA MONA CHUGUNA
and PAT LOWE

illustrated by MERVYN STREET

TIMOR SEA

INDIAN OCEAN

KIMBERLEY

BROOME

Fitzroy Crossing

Cherrabun Station

TANAMI DESERT

Walmajarri Country

GREAT SANDY DESERT

GIBSON DESERT

GREAT VICTORIA DESERT

THE WALMAJARRI PEOPLE

Walmajarri is one of several languages spoken by people whose homelands lie in the Great Sandy Desert, to the south of Fitzroy Crossing in Western Australia. Theirs is a country without borders, defined by the waterholes on which desert people's lives depended. The land is a vast dunefield of parallel jilji, or sandhills, which run in a roughly east-west direction, sometimes for hundreds of kilometres, broken by low outcrops of rocks.

Because of the isolation and dryness of the Great Sandy Desert, the Walmajarri were spared the fate of their nearest neighbours to the north, whose more fertile lands had been taken over by newcomers with herds of cattle and flocks of sheep.

They remained living freely in the desert until the lure of modern life gradually drew them, a few at a time, to the stations. By 1961, the Walmajarri Exodus was complete.

MANA AND HER RELATIONS

Jaja	Mana and Tili's grandmother, who had a bad back
Japi	Mana's youngest 'sister'
Kaj	Lilil and Miwa's husband
Kana	Yinti's younger brother, uncle to Mana, though younger than she is
Karli	Miwa's youngest son, about the same age as Kana
Kayi	Lilil's daughter, whom Mana calls 'sister'
Kurru	Mana's husband
Lilil	Yinti's sister, married to Kaj. Mana calls her 'Aunty'
Mala	Yinti's mother
Mana (2)	Dog with the same name as Mana
Miwa	Kaj's second wife
Pali	Mana's elder sister
Parri	Mana's blind mother's last son
Parta	Yinti's second mother
Riji	Miwa's elder son
Tili	Mana's younger sister
Yinti	Mana's uncle and age-mate

CONTENTS

INTRODUCTION

Jukuna Mona Chuguna

Jukuna told me these stories in Broome, between 2008 and 2011, when she was living in the hostel just around the corner from my house.

I had already known Jukuna for many years. The first time I met her was when she came to Broome with her husband, Kurrapakuta, in 1985, to visit her uncle and age-mate, Jimmy Pike, in Broome Regional Prison, where I was working as a psychologist. Pike, who was already gaining a reputation as an artist, was approaching the end of a long prison sentence, and his family was making plans for his release on parole, expected the following year. They had recently set up a tiny outstation on the edge of the desert they had all come from, and the plan was for Pike to serve his parole out there, away from the temptations of town. On one occasion, Jukuna and Kurrapakuta took me to visit their outstation, and I was surprised to see how basic it was: a bore for water, a couple of canvases for shelter, a fireplace, and little else. Their campsite, next to a mining track, was flat and dusty, surrounded by sand and spinifex.

I had no inkling at the time that, before the following year was out, I too would be living close to this outstation with Jimmy Pike, and getting to know Jukuna and her extended family really well. We shared hunting expeditions and Jukuna was a natural teacher, always ready to show and explain aspects of desert life.

Jukuna grew up in the Great Sandy Desert, with a family of hunters and gatherers, whose language was Walmajarri. Her life was like that of her ancestors, although there were already signs of another world outside the desert, where recently settled people with reddish skins now ruled. The stories that came back to the desert were mixed. On one hand, the newcomers could be harsh and unpredictable; on the other, they had created a life of greater security, mainly by providing food for people who worked for them. Hunting was no longer necessary during the working week, although it remained a favoured activity.

During the 1940s and 1950s, desert people began drifting towards the stations, first as fringe-dwellers, later as workers. Some kept in contact with their desert relations, walking back to the sandhill country during the wet season break from work, taking gifts such as tools and blankets, and bringing news about family members and station life. They might return to the station at the beginning of the following dry season, or choose to stay in the desert with their relations for another year until rain had fallen again, filling up the waterholes.

Jukuna's husband, Kurrapakuta, led his young bride out of the desert, to take up life on Cherrabun cattle station in the Kimberley. Both of them worked on the station and later moved to the Mission in the small town of Fitzroy Crossing, where Jukuna became a committed Christian. There the pair met two linguists, Joyce Hudson and Eirlys Richards, who were studying the Walmajarri language. Both Jukuna and Kurrapakuta helped Joyce and Eirlys to speak and analyse their language, and they themselves learnt to write it. They provided the linguists with stories in Walmajarri, which were published in small editions as the first books of readings for other people who wanted to learn to write their language.

In the 1980s, Karrayili Adult Education Centre was opened in Fitzroy Crossing, and Jukuna attended regularly, following classes in English literacy and starting to paint pictures. Not long afterwards the new art centre, Mangkaja Arts, was set up in the town, and Jukuna, along with her husband and many of their relations, took advantage of the new facilities to paint there. Jukuna developed her own style of painting: scenes from her desert country, with its waterholes, its trees and flowers. Her works were exhibited in Australia and overseas, and she travelled to France and England. I accompanied her to Brighton in 2003, and on one leg of the return journey a fuel line on our aircraft developed a leak, causing one of the two engines to emit explosive sounds and to be shut down. As we slowly turned around and returned to Kuching, Jukuna held my hand, closed her eyes and prayed. We landed safely.

Around the same time, Jukuna wrote her life story in Walmajarri, which was translated into English by Eirlys Richards and published in 2004, along with the story of her sister, Ngarta, in one volume called Two Sisters.

In later life, Jukuna suffered from diabetes and eventually kidney failure. She had to go to Perth for renal dialysis until there was a vacancy in Broome, where she continued receiving treatment three times a week and lived in the dialysis hostel, just around the corner from my house.

On most days when she didn't have to attend the dialysis centre, Jukuna would walk to my house to do her painting and share a cup of tea. She would sit at a table and work quietly and steadily, often completing a painting in one afternoon. She was so dedicated to her art that she sometimes ran out of canvases before I could order more from Mangkaja Arts in Fitzroy Crossing. On rare occasions when she didn't feel like painting, Jukuna would sit and tell me stories of her childhood in the desert, a time she remembered with nostalgia. I would write down her stories and, as the collection grew, I suggested that we should publish them in a book. Jukuna liked this idea, and tried to think of new stories to tell me.

At other times, especially in the cooler months, Jukuna liked to build a small fire in my yard and, sitting cross-legged on the ground in front of it, burn bark she had gathered; when the ashes were cool she scooped them into a small container and took them away for her hostel companions to mix with their chewing tobacco. When her friend Karen brought her a drum of ngarlka, desert nuts, from a field trip, Jukuna would cook some of them in the coals of her fire, just as she had done as a young woman. She would then spend hours breaking them open and putting the kernels into a tin to take home.

Over the two years she lived in the hostel, Jukuna suffered from frequent bouts of illness and was often admitted to hospital. I watched her grow frailer. She could still make her way to my house with the aid of a walking stick.

Although I wrote down Jukuna's stories in her own words, it was clear that they could not be published just as they were. She told them to me in her own, heavily Kriolised English, which would have been difficult for most readers to understand. Also, in telling them to me, Jukuna assumed a great deal of knowledge that the average reader would not have. In addition, some of the people in the stories were no longer living, and using their names was therefore not appropriate and would cause offence. I put it to Jukuna that we could overcome these difficulties if I rewrote her stories in the third person, and gave her characters different names, as I had done in earlier books I'd written with Jimmy Pike: Yinti and Desert Cowboy.

Jukuna immediately understood the problem, was happy with my proposal and helped me choose alternative names for the people in the stories. For historical interest, we kept all the original place-names. When I had drafted a new version I read some of it back to Jukuna. She didn't want to hear the whole thing — her English wasn't up to it — but she did get the idea and gave my efforts her blessing.

In 2011, Jukuna, whose health had been steadily deteriorating, died of complications from her diabetes. At her funeral in Fitzroy Crossing, many people spoke of her work in recording and teaching the Walmajarri language and telling stories. The present volume is her last contribution to the world of art and storytelling.

Pat Lowe
Broome 2015

'Jukuna' is now the accepted spelling of the author's personal name. It is pronounced with the 'u' sound in 'put', with the emphasis on the first syllable: Jukuna. Jukuna was given the English name 'Mona' on Cherrabun Station, in keeping with the practice of the times, and her own name was spelt 'Chuguna' and became her official surname. Her relations and friends have continued to call her Jukuna. However, Jukuna signed her paintings with her official name, 'Mona Chuguna'.

BEFORE CONTACT

The history of Aboriginal people since Europeans first arrived in Australia has been very different from one part of the country to the other. The east and south of the continent were settled first, and the impact on Aboriginal people who lived in those areas was huge. The north and west of the continent were settled much later, while the central deserts were considered too hot and arid for white settlement and were only visited by a handful of explorers, a number of whom lost their lives on their journeys. Aboriginal people in the deserts were, for the most part, left in peace to continue their age-old, stable existence as semi-nomadic hunters and gatherers. So it was that Jukuna grew up in the Great Sandy Desert, not leaving until she was a young married woman, in around 1960.

Many details about the way people lived in the desert will be found in Jukuna's stories, but some explanations may help the reader to understand them better.

MANA

Mana was born under a tree. The country she grew up in was wide as the sky, and the sun shone hot for most of the year. In every direction was sand: deep, red, warm sand that showed the footprints of every creature that walked on it; people, dogs, lizards, snakes, insects, all left their marks. At night, Mana went to sleep under a myriad stars.

When Mana was small, she was surrounded by her family: her mother, her older sister, her father and his second wife all camped together. At night, she slept on the sand beside her parents in their windbreak. During the day, her mother carried her everywhere in a wooden coolamon. While her mother gathered food, Mana lay in her coolamon in the shade of a nearby tree and when she got hungry, her mother fed her from her breast.

When Mana grew too big for the coolamon, her mother carried her on her hip while she walked and sat Mana down in the shade, on the soft sand, while she was working.

Little Mana watched her mother collect seeds from the bushes. She listened to the birds and looked at the lizards and insects in the spinifex. She noticed the

different patterns made by their feet. She toddled around on the sand or sat and played with leaves that had fallen from the trees.

When Mana was a little older, she was often cared for by her grandmother while the other grown-ups went hunting and looking for food. Her grandmother was her mother's mother, so Mana called her Jaja.

The family didn't stay in one place for very long. They would camp for a while on a sandhill near a waterhole and go hunting every day from there. When they weren't able to catch so many animals, they would move to somewhere else.

Mana's father would pick up his spears and hunting sticks, his wives would carry their digging sticks in their hands and wooden coolamons of water on their heads. One of the women would lift Mana onto her shoulders and everyone would set off, stopping to gather food or hunt an animal on the way.

Often, other people joined Mana's little family group: aunties, uncles and cousins would come and camp nearby, or Mana's family would find relations at the next waterhole. And so Mana learnt about her country and got to know all the people who lived in it.

RELATIONSHIPS

Desert men often had more than one wife, and the wives called one another 'sister'. The women shared the care of their children, who called all their father's wives 'mother'. Jukuna therefore speaks of her 'own' and her 'second' mother, to distinguish them in her stories.

Aboriginal people have many relationship terms, and use different names for their mother's mother and their father's mother (as well as different terms for their mother's and father's fathers). In Walmajarri, Jukuna's language, one's mother's mother is 'jaja' and father's mother is 'ngawiji'. These terms are reciprocal – that is, the grandchildren are called 'jaja' and 'ngawiji' as well. This is why Aboriginal people speaking English often refer to their grandchildren as their 'grannies'.

Getting Food

Desert people gathered all their own food and hunted animals for meat. When grass and wattle seeds were in season, women gathered them and ground them up on rocks with water into a smooth paste, which they cooked in the coals to make a type of dark, unleavened bread.

Women carried the food they gathered in large wooden dishes or coolamons, usually made by their husbands. They used deep coolamons to carry water when they were travelling far from camp. Shallow coolamons were used for carrying babies.

Other tools used by desert people included spears, made from tall, straight saplings, and hunting sticks, carved out of hardwood, shaped and smoothed. Spears were men's weapons, but women sometimes used them as well. Women more often carried long digging sticks, with which they probed the ground to find yams or to trace an animal's burrow. Both men and women used hunting sticks to kill or knock down prey from trees.

WATER

Water in the desert was scarce. There was no surface water except here and there in claypans and rockholes during a good wet season. For most of the year, people got water from wells or waterholes they dug at known places in the sand, often a day's walk or more from one another, and they had to remember exactly where these places were. Each waterhole had a name, and people always made their main camps near waterholes. Small family groups spent each year walking across the desert from one waterhole to another, guided by their knowledge of the country and its resources. They would base themselves at one place for a time, living off the land around them, then move on to a new waterhole when food began to get scarce.

The most important waterholes were the jila, because they never ran dry. Even in the driest time of year, people knew that if they dug out a jila, they would always find water. Other waterholes held water after rain, but eventually they would dry up.

A jila was usually the home of a spirit snake, which kept the water there and could affect the weather, bringing rain or storms. Some such snakes travelled under the ground, rearing their heads in different places, called japi.

LANTIMANGU

Mana got her name from a place called Lantimangu, where the sandhill is smooth, without grass or bushes growing on it. Lantimangu is a japi, where the waterhole snake comes up from under the ground and looks out. It's also a place where wurruwurru, spirit babies, live.

Before Mana was born, her mother and father were hunting near Lantimangu when her mother came across a desert nut tree with a lot of nice soft gum oozing from a break in the bark. She ate some of the gum and collected more to share with her family later.

Around the same time, the couple had a dream. 'Ah, maybe we're going to have a baby!' they said. When the baby was born, they called her Mana, after the tree with that gum. Mana is her jarriny, her spirit.

When Mana was a baby, her Jaja often looked after her, and when she was hungry, Jaja gave her milk from her breast. The older woman would sit by the fire and hold her breasts in the smoke to help them make milk. She also rubbed them with the milky sap of a small shrub.

Even when Mana grew bigger, she still loved to go everywhere with her Jaja.

One day, when Mana was still a little girl, Jaja took her and her elder sister, Pali, to gather food near Lantimangu. They set off walking in the early morning and reached Lantimangu in the afternoon. They sat down in a soft hollow in a sandhill. 'We can camp here,' Jaja said.

While Pali and Mana gathered wood to make a fire, Jaja went off to pick some of the wirtuka they had come for. Wirtuka is the root of a yellow plant that grows along the ground near a waterhole.

Pali lit the dry grass and wood with her jarra, the firestick she had been carrying, and soon had a good little fire crackling.

By the time Jaja came back carrying a heap of wirtuka in her coolamon, Mana was hungry. She didn't want to wait.

'Jaja, you cook some wirtuka for me first, and you two can have some later,' she said.

'No,' said Jaja. 'We're all going to have it later on, for supper.'

Mana started crying. 'No, I want some now! Cook it for me, I'm hungry!'

Jaja sighed. She sat down on the sand near the fire, raked some of the hot coals to one side and cooked some of the wirtuka to satisfy Mana. Later, when the sun had sunk to the horizon and the fire had burnt down to coals, Jaja cooked the rest of the wirtuka for herself and Pali.

Soon, it was dark and they all went to sleep under the vast sky, in the glow of the red coals.

That night, Mana had a disturbing dream. She dreamed that her spirit brother at Lantimangu was chasing her with a kurra, a stone axe. He tried to hit her with it, but Mana was too quick for him and got away.

At dawn, Jaja got up and went down to the waterhole to fill her coolamon. She too had had a bad dream, she told Mana later. A little boy had chased her with a kurra too.

After filling her coolamon with water and leaving it in the camp, Jaja started gathering more wirtuka from the ground near the waterhole.

Pali and Mana woke up and had a drink of water from the coolamon. They could see their grandmother working down in the flat, not far away. Suddenly, she gave a cry of pain and fell down, lifeless.

Pali went running down the side of the sandhill and across the flat to her grandmother, who was lying on the ground, not moving. Mana followed.

'Jaja, what's wrong? What have you done?' cried Pali.

'Oh!' groaned Jaja. 'That wurruwurru grandson hit me with a kurra. "Why are you stealing my food?" he said. "That's mine!" Then he knocked me hard on the back. I can't get up, I'm in too much pain.'

Pali lifted her grandmother and helped her into the shade. Mana held Jaja in her arms while Pali stripped some bark from a yakapiri bush and tied it around Jaja's waist, to support her back. Jaja lay still and after a while she went to sleep.

SPIRIT CHILDREN

Most of the named places in the desert are waterholes, but Lantimangu is a japi. It is a smooth sandhill, known to be a place where spirit babies live.

Every baby born in the desert has a spirit, which enters it at the time the mother first realises she is pregnant. Around that time she or her husband usually has a vivid dream, often about an animal but sometimes a plant, which they take to represent the jarriny, or spirit of the coming child. They may recently have killed the same kind of animal as in the dream, or gathered the same plants, releasing the baby's spirit. Sometimes, a child is given the name of its jarriny, as Mana was.

Spirit babies live in certain places, each waiting for a human mother, but not all of them find one. Jukuna's 'spirit brother' in the same story never became a human child. The family knew he was living at Lantimangu because of what happened to Jukuna's grandmother.

Pali and Mana waited anxiously beside her, talking quietly.

When she woke up, the girls asked her, 'Are you all right now, Jaja?' Her spine was still very sore, so Pali carried her on her back all the way to the next waterhole, Mantarta.

Later in the afternoon, the rest of the family came back to Mantarta with the animals and nuts they had got. The girls' father could see there was something wrong.

'What's the matter with your grandmother?' he asked them. He couldn't speak to the old woman directly because she was his mother-in-law. The girls told him what had happened.

Jaja kept the yakapiri tied around her waist for three days. When she felt better she took it off. It was the

MAKING MILK

In some cultures, women share the breastfeeding of babies. Other women who have recently had a baby of their own may feed another one, and sometimes, older women are able to produce milk as well. Jukuna's Jaja fed her granddaughter and she used bush medicine to keep her breasts full of milk. Smoke was used to heal wounds and treat ailments as well as to strengthen babies and, as in this case, to stimulate the production of milk. Often people who were sick simply sat or lay near a fire and allowed the smoke to blow towards them, but sometimes people burnt branches from medicinal trees and 'smoked' themselves or others with them.

second time she had hurt her back; the first time, she had fallen out of a tree, but she was only sore for a while. After that attack at Lantimangu, she always suffered from a bad back.

The family never went back to Lantimangu after that because they knew that Mana's bad-tempered spirit brother was there, waiting in a cave. He was never born as a human being, as the girls had been. He just stayed there at Lantimangu, a grumpy spirit.

DESERT PLANTS

One staple food in the desert was the nut from the Turtujarti tree (Desert Walnut, *Owenia reticulata*), whose bark, when cut or damaged, yields a soft, edible gum that crystallises over time into a crunchy substance, which becomes sticky when chewed. Turtujarti nuts can lie under a tree in their hard shells for a long time before they go rotten, and could therefore be relied upon when other food was scarce.

Yakapiri (Bird-flower Bush, *Crotalaria cunninghamii*) is a shrub that grows in sandy country. It has a soft bark that can be torn off in strips and plaited to make sandals to protect the feet from hot sand, or used as a cord or tie, as in this story.

WHAT ARE KARTIYA LIKE?

One day, Mana was gathering flowers for nectar with her grandmother when the old woman started telling her a story:

A long time ago, we were camping at the jila, Kulyayi. One morning, we women all went off together to gather food and honey. When we got back to the jila in the afternoon, we found two kartiya there, with their camels. They had two camels, one for riding, one for carrying things. They had canvas too.

The men came back from hunting around the same time.

"Hey," we said to one another. "Who's that at the waterhole? We can't go down there!" We were frightened. The kartiya had killed a big snake and put it in the sun.

"Ah, what are we going to do? Where can we get water?"

"We'll have to go somewhere else; these kartiya might grab us!"

"No, we don't want to go a long way, to another place."

When the kartiya had finished drinking, we went down to the jila to look for water. Nothing! Those kartiya and their camels had taken it all! There was only a little drop left. They'd killed the jila snake too, so no more water was coming up.

The kartiya cooked the snake and offered it to us. "You lot want snake?"

"No, we can't eat that snake." We felt sorry for that snake and about losing our precious water.

Then the kartiya wanted more water.

"No, we've got no water here," we told them. The kartiya had taken it all.

'What are kartiya like?' Mana asked her granny. 'What do kartiya look like?'

'Kartiya?' said Jaja. 'Kartiya are red, you know. They are big red people.'

'What sort of red?' Mana asked her. 'Red like blood?'

'Yes, that's right.'

'Are they like animals?' Mana wanted to know.

'No,' said her grandmother. 'They are like people. They have a face, like a person. They've got two eyes, everything.'

Mana thought about this. She tried to imagine what a kartiya might look like. She pictured them as giants.

'Are they big, like someone from the Dreamtime?' Mana asked again.

'No, they're not from the Dreamtime. They are real people, like us, only different. Different colour.'

KARTIYA

'Kartiya' is a name widely used across the Kimberley for people of European origin ('white' people). Very few had ventured into Walmajarri country, but those explorers who did so usually rode camels, which were more suited to the sandy country than horses. Jukuna's grandmother and members of her family had this strange encounter with a couple of men with camels. They had never seen kartiya or camels before and didn't know what to make of them.

TWO BROTHERS

Mana had an aunty, Lilil, who was around when Mana was small, with Lilil's younger brothers, Yinti and Kana. When Lilil was old enough, she married a man named Kaj, and left the desert with him to work on a cattle station. Kaj later took a second wife, Miwa. In the wet season, during holiday time on the station, Kaj sometimes brought Lilil and Miwa and their young children back to the desert to visit their families.

While Kaj and his wives were back living in the desert, Mana sometimes went hunting or gathering food with Miwa. One time, Miwa took Pali and Mana to gather kumpupaja, leaving Miwa's two little sons, Riji and Karli, with their other mother, Lilil.

'Can we come?' the boys asked.

'No,' Miwa told them. 'It's too far for you and we don't want to carry you when you get tired.'

After their mother had gone with the two girls, the little boys decided to follow them but they didn't tell anyone they were going.

When Lilil noticed the boys were missing, she thought, 'Maybe they are playing near the waterhole. I'll go and look for them.' She walked down the sandhill to

the waterhole, where the boys had been playing earlier, but they weren't there. She started to follow their tracks.

'Ah, the two boys went that way, after the others,' she thought.

Lilil went back and filled up a small coolamon with water and set off to follow the two boys. It was a hot day and she was worried about them. She didn't think they would be able to catch up with the girls and she knew they had no water with them.

After walking for a good way, Lilil spotted Riji standing up under a little bush. When she got closer, she saw that little Karli was lying down, resting. She hurried up to them.

'Get up now,' Lilil told Karli. 'Come and drink some water.'

The boys were hot and thirsty from their walk and both drank eagerly from the coolamon. Then Lilil took them back to camp, stopping in the shade several times to let them rest. When they all got back, Lilil took the boys over to the waterhole, made them sit down and sprinkled water on them to cool them down.

'Why did you two go running off?' she asked them.

'We were following Mummy,' said Riji. 'She went with the girls to get kumpupaja and left us behind.'

When Kaj came back from hunting, the boys were still weak and the women told him what had happened. He was angry with his wives.

'Why did you let the boys wander away on their own?' he wanted to know. 'They could have died of thirst!'

'Don't blame me!' Lilil told him. 'I'm the one who went looking for them. I kept them alive and brought them back!'

Kaj got angry with Miwa then. 'You shouldn't have left them behind!' He raised his hunting stick and gave her a whack across her back, making her cry. Lilil stood between her husband and Miwa and told him to stop hitting his young wife. He walked off, grumbling.

Karli was sick, vomiting all night. But by the next morning, he was better. By then, the grown-ups had got over their bad feelings.

STATION PEOPLE

When Mana was growing up, many desert people were leaving the sandhills and moving to cattle stations. Sometimes, relations came back to the desert, bringing presents, and took up the old life for a while, as Kaj and Lilil did.

DANGER

While children were free to play and run around in the sandhills, if they wandered too far from camp they were in danger of dying of thirst. This was especially true in the hot weather, when the early morning may seem cool, but the sun soon becomes fiercely hot and the ground can burn your feet. In such weather, it doesn't take long to get very thirsty.

KUMPUPAJA

Kumpupaja are the greenish fruit of a small shrub, (Solanum sp.), which ripen in the dry season. They are full of bitter black seeds, which have to be scraped out before the fruit can be eaten.

MANA'S BLIND MOTHER

Mana had two mothers. Her own mother was her father's first wife, and his second wife was blind. When the family moved from one waterhole to another, someone had to lead the young blind woman, holding one end of a stick while the blind woman followed, holding the other end. Mana often led her.

The blind woman had once left the desert. She had travelled with her mother north to a cattle station, where she was given to her promised husband, who was working there.

She was a good-looking girl, with long black hair, and another man saw her and wanted her for himself. Tensions rose and the two men fought over her.

The girl's promised husband won the fight and kept his wife, but having a blind wife wasn't easy. She couldn't do the sort of work a wife was expected to do, and he had to look after her.

The blind girl's husband came back to the desert to visit his relations, bringing his wife with him. When it was time for him to return to his work on the station,

he gave his wife to Mana's father. 'You can have her,' he said. 'She's already been the cause of too much trouble on the station. I don't want to keep fighting over her.'

Mana's father accepted the young blind woman as his wife and Mana's mother looked after her, helped her and gave her food. When Mana was small, her blind mother would sometimes carry her.

Mana's blind mother often stayed behind at the waterhole to look after the children when the other adults went hunting. She couldn't go hunting herself, but she knew how to cook food and she could always hear where the children were and what they were up to.

Once, Mana's father was away from camp and her mother with the good eyes had gone to gather nuts, leaving Mana behind with her blind mother. Mana had been eating a lot of insects, puyurruyurru, and started to feel sick. Her blind mother was sitting nearby and Mana was so weak she fell on top of her.

'What's wrong with you?' her blind mother asked, but Mana couldn't tell her, she was vomiting so much.

Her blind mother took Mana into her arms and held her, stroking her head. 'Hey,' she said. 'How are you feeling now?'

By evening, Mana was feeling better.

Over the years, Mana's blind mother had four babies, three boys and a girl. Sadly, all except one of the boys died while they were still infants. Mana didn't know why they had died, and she wondered if perhaps her blind mother hadn't had enough milk to feed them. Everyone loved the last little boy, who was called Parri.

MARRIAGE

Girls were usually promised in marriage to an older man, sometimes when they were babies or even before they were born; for instance, a man might promise another man his first daughter. The girls were introduced to their future husbands while they were young, to get to know them. Although most young women did marry their promised husbands, sometimes one of them ran away, or another man might come along and steal her. If either of these things happened, the wronged husband would have the right to punish his wife and the other man, but once that had happened, the runaways often stayed together. More rarely, a man might offer his wife to another man, as in this story, following a dispute over her.

TWO LITTLE GIRLS

One day in the hot-weather time, when the whole family was camping at Mantarta, all the grown-ups and Pali went hunting. Mana, her younger sister Tili and another little 'sister' called Japi stayed behind with Jaja, who still had a bad back.

Mana was helping her grandmother to test some of the nuts she had gathered earlier. Her two young sisters came to watch. Mana used a heavy hunting stick to crack the shells, then broke them open with her hands. If too many of the kernels were stale or rotten, the whole pile would have to be thrown away.

'Can we have some nuts, Jaja?' asked Tili.

'Not yet, we haven't tested them. We're going to cook them later, when everyone comes home from hunting.'

'Well, we're going to look for fruit, Jaja,' said Tili.

'No, it's too hot, you're not to go wandering off.'

'But there's nothing to eat!'

'Never mind. Your parents will come back with plenty of meat.'

'We'll go and get some water, then,' said Tili.

Tili and Japi went to fetch two coolamons, one bigger than the other, and took them down to the waterhole. Tili filled the bigger one with water, then she glanced around; their grandmother and older sister were out of sight. She looked at little Japi. 'Come on,' she told her. 'We're going!'

Tili made a circlet of grass and put it on her head as a soft pad. Then she lifted the heavy wooden coolamon of water onto the grass pad and gave the smaller, empty one to Japi to carry.

The two sisters set off together. After a while, they found a shady tree.

'We'll leave the water here in the shade,' said Tili.

The sun was higher now, and hot, and Japi was starting to flag.

The girls had a long drink of water then left the coolamon under the tree and walked on. Japi was soon tired again, so Tili lifted her up and carried her on her back. When they came to a patch of ripe kumpupaja, they stopped and sat down. Together they pulled the kumpupaja off their prickly stems and put them into the small coolamon.

Meanwhile, at the camp, Pali had come back from hunting. She looked around for the younger girls.

'Jaja,' she said. 'Where have my two little sisters gone?'

'They went down to get water, but they've been gone for a long time. You'd better go and look for them.'

Pali went to look near the waterhole but no one was there. She saw the girls' tracks going away over the sand.

'No,' she said, when she came back. 'They're not there, they've gone off somewhere. Jaja, I'll follow them. It's hot now, they might get weak.'

Mana told Pali she'd go with her. The pair followed the tracks of their young sisters. After walking for a while over the hot sand, Pali sat down in the shade to rest. Mana kept going and before long she found the coolamon of water the girls had left under a tree. She drank some of the water and went on. Pali soon caught up with her.

Now they could only see Tili's tracks. 'Where's that little girl?' Mana asked.

'Tili must be carrying her,' said Pali. True enough, Tili's tracks were sinking deeper into the sand.

When Pali and Mana found their young sisters, the girls had collected a big pile of kumpupaja and were getting ready to walk back to their water in the shade.

'What have you two been up to?' Mana asked them. 'We've all been worried about you; it's a hot day!'

'No, we're all right,' said Tili. 'We've been picking all this fruit.'

TRACKING

In the desert, people followed the tracks of animals when they were hunting, or, as in this story, found missing children by following their tracks. There is more to tracking than following or finding something. People can tell by the depth of tracks if someone is carrying a heavy weight. They can also tell how old tracks are and how long ago an animal passed by. They can read a series of tracks like a story: when the animal was walking or running, when it stopped to rest or caught and ate another animal, whether it was a young or old, male or female and so on.

'Come on, we'd better take you two back to camp now,' said Pali. 'Jaja will be looking for us.'

They stopped to drink some water, then Pali put the empty coolamon on her head and lifted little Japi onto her back. Mana carried the girls' dish, full of fruit, and they all made their way slowly back to camp.

'Jaja,' Pali said. 'I've brought the two girls back safely; here they are.'

Jaja was crying, she'd been so worried. 'Why did you take your little sister away with you?' she asked Tili. 'She can't walk so far, she's too small. Her legs aren't strong enough yet.'

'We were hungry,' said Tili, 'and there was no fruit here. Look, we've brought back all these kumpupaja. I carried Japi when she got tired.'

Later that day, the girls' parents came back with the animals they'd killed: goanna and cat. They built up the fire, and while they were waiting for the meat, Jaja cooked the kumpupaja and nuts in the coals. Then everyone had a good feed and Tili was forgiven.

GOANNAS

Goannas are Varanus lizards of several species. In Jukuna's country, the most common is the sand goanna (*Varanus gouldii*). Others are the rough-tailed goanna (*Varanus acanthurus*) and the black-tailed goanna (*Varanus tristis*).

NO WATER

When Mana was small, she heard the story of her other grandmother, her father's mother, whom she had never met. The events had all happened long before Mana was born.

It was hot-weather time, and people were travelling and burning the grass as they went, to clear the ground for walking and hunting. They had run out of water and everyone was getting thirsty, so they started hurrying on to the next waterhole. The old lady tried to keep up with the others, but the heat nearly overcame her.

'Keep going just till we get to the next jumu,' the others encouraged her. They helped her along to the waterhole, only to find it dry.

'There's no water,' her son said, looking worried. 'It hasn't rained here for a long time. We'll have to keep going.'

'I can't go any further,' his mother told the other people. 'You go and find water and bring some back to me.'

The old woman sank to the ground under a small tree, but it was the middle of the day and there wasn't a lot of shade. She waited there for a long time; her throat was parched.

The others kept going until at last they reached the next jila and drank all the water they could. After a short rest, Mana's mother filled her wooden coolamon and lifted it onto her head. Then she carried it all the way back to where they'd left her mother-in-law. The old woman was still lying there in the same position under the same spindly tree, but the shadow would have moved away from her during the afternoon, leaving her in the full sun. By now, it was evening.

When Mana's mother saw that the old woman hadn't moved, she called out her mother-in-law's name. There was no answer. As she drew close, Mana's mother saw that the old woman was no longer breathing. She had died of thirst.

WATERHOLES

In the desert, where the heat can be intense and waterholes are often far apart, people had to think about water whenever they left camp. We have seen that they often carried water with them, in wooden coolamons, while they were hunting or travelling.

Desert people had to plan longer journeys according to where they would find water. The jila were always reliable, but the jumu eventually ran dry between one rainy season and another. In the dry season, travellers sometimes had to take an educated guess as to whether a particular jumu would still have water in it or not. They knew the ones that usually lasted longer than others, and they took note of rain, even distant thunderstorms, and could tell which waterholes were likely to be replenished.

Occasionally, someone would make a mistake; the water they were carrying would run out before they had got close to the next waterhole, and there would be a long and thirsty walk. By resting in the shade during the hottest part of the day and walking in the cooler evenings and mornings, people usually made it to safety. The danger was greater for old or sick people who could not keep up with the younger ones, and the desert showed no mercy to those left behind.

UNCLE YINTI

Yinti was the same age as Mana and his younger brother, Kana, was about the same age as Tili. Mana and Tili called the boys 'uncle'. Their two families often travelled around and camped together, and the children knew each other well.

The girls liked having Yinti around because he was so much fun, but he was always getting into trouble.

One afternoon, when most of the adults had gone hunting, Jaja stayed behind at the waterhole with all the kids. Jaja told them to go and gather food.

'Go and collect some jurnta, children, then we'll cook them,' Jaja said.

But Mana didn't feel like gathering jurnta.

'No,' she said. 'We can get some later.'

She stayed back, but all the other kids, girls and boys, ran down to the flat. They sat on the ground, digging by hand for the tasty little bulbs. When they had collected a big pile, they took them back to Jaja.

'Now you can cook them,' said Jaja.

Mana was still in a contrary mood. 'No, you cook them for us, Jaja,' she said.

Jurnta

Jurnta is another desert food, a type of grass that grows on salty ground. People gathered and ate the small greyish-white bulbs, which they dug up by hand from the base of their stems. Jurnta can be eaten raw or lightly cooked in the coals.

'Alright,' said Jaja. 'You all go and play now, down on the flat.'

The children didn't need telling twice. They all ran off, leaving Jaja in the shade, cooking jurnta.

Mana played in the flat with Tili and their cousin Kayi, Lilil's daughter. Yinti, Kana and the other boys were throwing boomerangs nearby. They were light ones they'd made themselves out of bark.

Tili and Kayi kept running up and down in the middle of the flat. Mana told them not to run around like that in case they got hit by a boomerang, but the younger girls took no notice.

Yinti threw a boomerang just as Kayi was running out, and the boomerang flew round and caught her, crack! right on the bridge of her nose. Kayi fell to the ground, blood pouring. Yinti and the other boys took off running and Jaja, who had seen what had happened, tried to chase them. She shook her walking stick at their fleeing backs.

'Come here! Come back here! Don't run away — when I get hold of you lot I'm going to hit you with my stick!'

But the boys kept going. The girls were all crying; Kayi was crying because she'd been hurt and was bleeding, and Tili and Mana were crying for Kayi.

Later that day, Kayi's father and mother, and Yinti's two mothers, Mala and Parta, came in from hunting. Mana and Tili told them what had happened and they saw that Kayi's nose was bleeding and sore.

When it was starting to get dark and the boys came creeping back to camp, Kayi's father Kaj gave them a good growling.

'We didn't mean to hit her,' said Yinti. 'She ran out just when I was throwing a boomerang.' Mana wasn't so sure. She had a feeling Yinti had thrown the boomerang on purpose.

By then, Kayi's nose had stopped bleeding but her face had swollen up. She soon got better, but she carried a scar on her nose for the rest of her life — a reminder of Yinti.

BOOMERANGS

Boomerangs are curved weapons made from hard wood, carefully cut and smoothed. Throwing boomerangs are used for killing prey, such as kangaroos, and others for ceremonies and for fighting. A heavy boomerang thrown at a human being could cause serious, even lethal injury.

Children made toy weapons from lighter materials such as the bark of trees, and practised throwing or mock-fighting with them. Even so, a bark boomerang thrown with some force could do damage.

THE CUTTING

When Mana was a girl, people used to cut one another across their chests and sometimes on their upper arms, to decorate themselves with scars.

One day, when all the kids were playing in the sandhills, away from the camp, Yinti came along, holding a sharp flake of stone in his hand.

'Line up, all you girls!' Yinti told Mana and her companions, Tili and Kayi. He made them sit on the ground in a line, then he said, 'I'm going to cut you. It will be good for you.'

Tili and Kayi were frightened. 'No, don't cut us!' they begged him. 'It will hurt!'

'Yes, I'll cut you, it's good for you. If you don't let me cut you, the bad kukurr spirit might get you — he'll bite you! But if he sees you've got a scar, he'll leave you alone.'

Yinti told the boys to stand on one side and wait. He sat down on the ground in front of the girls and gave each of them a nick on the arm with his stone knife. Then he made a bigger cut across their chests.

'Pain, pain! That hurts!' the girls cried, but Yinti took no notice. Soon, blood was running down their bodies and all the girls were in tears.

When he had finished with the girls, Yinti made the boys stand up and started doing the same to them. He cut Riji and Karli and even his own little brother Kana. The boys were soon crying too.

'You mustn't cry,' Yinti told them. 'You should laugh! You have to be brave and strong!'

When Yinti had finished cutting them, the kids all ran back to camp, their tears mingling with the blood pouring down their arms and chests.

Jaja saw them first.

'Warawu!' she cried out. 'Whatever happened to you all, girls and boys?' They told her what Yinti had done to them. He sat down on the sand a little way off, smirking to himself, pretending not to be listening.

Jaja was furious. 'Wait till your mother comes back!' she told Yinti.

Pali was the first to come back from hunting. When she heard what had happened and saw the state the children were in, she scolded Yinti.

'What have you done to the little kids? That's wrong, you shouldn't have done that!'

When the mothers came home to camp and heard what Yinti had been doing, they picked up their digging sticks and went to hit him, but he was too quick for them. He jumped up and took off, running.

The children, meanwhile, had rubbed themselves with charcoal from the fire to stop the bleeding and dry up the wounds.

Yinti stayed away from camp for the rest of the day and didn't come back till it was nearly dark. Then the old people gave him a big telling off.

'You shouldn't do that — you shouldn't cut little boys and girls!' said Jaja. 'You're mad, you hurt them!' She kept telling him off all night.

'Are you crazy or what?' said Mana and Tili's mother.

'No,' said Yinti. 'Those little kids asked me to cut them, desert way.'

'Rubbish,' said Pali. 'They never asked you to do that.'

Mana's blind mother chimed in too: 'Why did you cut the little kids?'

All the kids carried Yinti's scars on their bodies for the rest of their lives. When they grew up they sometimes showed off their scars and told the story, laughing and laughing, while Yinti smiled sheepishly.

BODY SCARS

Not all societies are afraid of a degree of pain and bleeding, and in many cultures, people decorate their bodies by scarification or cutting. Most desert people had lines cut across their chests, which they rubbed with ash and ochre to raise the scars into ridges. Some added to these chest scars by cutting patterns all over their arms or torsos. Usually, this was done when people were considered old enough and wanted to have themselves cut.

BLACKNOSE

Mana and Tili had a dog named Blacknose. They called her 'mother' because she had the same skin name as their mothers. Their mother called the dog 'sister'. Blacknose was a good hunter.

One day, the two sisters went gathering food. They didn't take Blacknose because she had already been hunting with their parents and was hot and tired, so she stayed behind at the waterhole.

When they came back to camp in the afternoon, the girls saw their uncle Yinti walking away with his spears. It was unusual for him to be going hunting so late, when everyone else was coming home. His little brother Kana was still there at the camp.

Blacknose didn't come running to greet the girls, wagging her tail, as she usually did.

'Where's Blacknose?' asked Mana.

Kana seemed excited.

'Your dog's over there,' he said, pointing. 'Up in that tree. Yinti put her there!'

'Can't be!' Mana and Tili hurried over to look. They found poor Blacknose dead, hanging over a fork in the tree, her tongue lolling. Blood had run from a

wound in her body, but now it was dry. She'd been speared.

'Who killed our dog?' the girls asked Kana, but they had already guessed. Tili started to cry.

'Yinti killed her,' Kana told them. 'Your dog was in the waterhole when we came back from hunting. We were thirsty, but she wouldn't let us get water. She snarled at us when we tried to chase her out. Yinti set fire to some grass and threw it at her, and then she jumped out and ran away.'

'Well, why did he kill her?' Mana wanted to know.

'He was still wild with her,' Kana said. 'After we'd had a drink of water and a rest, he followed her tracks and found her under a tree, asleep. That's when he speared her.'

When it was getting dark, Yinti came back to camp.

'Who killed our dog?' the girls asked him. He didn't say anything, but just grinned guiltily and pointed at Kana. Kana shook his head.

'No, it was you!' Mana said. 'Why did you just hang her up in a tree; why didn't you cook her and eat her?' she asked him, sarcastically. She never quite forgave Yinti for killing Blacknose.

DOGS

Dogs were important to desert people for hunting and companionship, just as they are today. They are treated as members of the family and fit into the relationship structure like human beings. These relationships are taken seriously; if a woman has a dog she calls 'sister', the woman's children call the dog 'mother', as they would call their mother's human sister, and the dog's offspring become the woman's 'sons' and 'daughters' and her children's 'brothers' and 'sisters'.

Because desert people valued their dogs highly, it was a serious offence to kill another person's dog. Only if a dog attacked and bit someone was it considered reasonable for the injured person to kill it, as a dangerous animal. In this story, Mana and Tili don't consider Yinti to have been justified in killing their dog, even though Blacknose had snarled at him and prevented him from getting water.

Nearly Buried Alive

One day, Kana and Karli were nearly buried alive.

It was hot-weather time and a lot of people were camping at one waterhole. The hole was deep, and the water was a long way down. When people were digging it out, they cut out steps in the steep, sandy sides for people to climb up and down.

The two boys, Kana and his nephew Karli, went to the waterhole together to have a drink. Kana's mothers and father were sitting in the shade of a tree, some way off. His brother Yinti had gone off hunting early and hadn't come back yet.

When the boys had been gone for a long time, Kana's father said to his younger wife, 'Where are those two boys?'

'I don't know where they've got to,' said Parta. 'I'll go and look for them. I'll get us some water at the same time.'

Parta picked up her empty coolamon and walked down towards the waterhole. She could see no sign of the boys and thought they must have wandered off to

chase lizards. As she went down the sandhill, she kept an eye out for the boys' tracks. When she got close to the waterhole, she saw that one side had caved in, covering up the water in the bottom and leaving a big gap in the sandy wall. She saw the boys' footprints at the top of the waterhole, where they had been standing before they went down for water, but no footprints coming out.

'The sand's fallen in on them!' Parta said to herself.

Quickly, she climbed down into the waterhole. As she did so, she saw movement under the sand. She felt around, grabbed hold of someone's arm and pulled one of the boys free. It was Karli, coughing and gasping for air. His face was grey with sand. Parta started digging with her coolamon, till she felt another movement:

Kana. She seized him with both hands and gave him a great heave, lifting him up beside her. His eyes and mouth were full of sand, and he sat spitting it out.

Parta helped both boys climb out of the waterhole. When she was sure they were all right, she told them to sit down in the shade of a nearby wattle tree and wait while she went back into the waterhole to dig the dirt out again. Using her coolamon, she scooped up the pile of sand that had fallen in and threw it out of the hole until she reached the shallow water in the bottom. She filled up her coolamon with water, then called out to the boys to help her. Kana, who was fast recovering, came to the top of the waterhole and looked in.

'Help me bring up this water,' Parta told him. Kana climbed part of the way down into the waterhole, fearful of slipping in again and landing on top of his mother. She raised the heavy coolamon as high as she could and passed it to Kana, who lifted it higher again and placed it on the sand at the top of the waterhole. Then he stepped out and Parta climbed up behind him.

When the three of them had had a rest, they all got up and went to join the other people in the shade near the top of the sandhill.

'These fellows nearly got buried alive!' Parta told the people waiting there.

When Kana's father heard what had happened, he growled at the boys. 'Don't play around inside a waterhole,' he told them. 'It's dangerous!'.

DIGGING FOR WATER

Desert waterholes are like wells and some are much deeper than others, especially when the water level has dropped during the dry season. To reach water in the deeper ones, as people dug down in the sand they cut footholds into the sides of the wells. If the upper part of a well was dry, the sand was likely to be soft and, if someone put weight on the side, it could cave in. For this reason, and to keep the water clean, children were discouraged from playing in the waterhole.

FIGHTING

When tempers flared, it was not unusual for people to hit one another and there were 'rules' about how people fought. If a man felt wronged, he might threaten another man with his boomerang and spears. If the wrong was serious, the offender was expected to take his punishment without resisting. Women who were fighting might use their hunting or digging stick to take turns to hit one another on the head. Relations would eventually intervene to stop a serious fight.

THE FIGHT

One night in the cold weather, all the kids had gone to sleep on the sand behind their windbreak. Small fires were burning close by, to keep them warm. The sky was clear and filled with stars, but a chilly wind was blowing.

Suddenly, the children woke up to hear the grown-ups shouting. Kaj was there with his two wives, and the argument was between his young wife, Miwa, and Yinti and Lilil's mother, Mala.

Sitting up, Mana saw Mala hit Miwa, and then Parta, Yinti's second mother, stood up for Miwa. They were all milling around in the dark, with just the firelight shining on their skin. The kids had no idea what they were fighting about.

All the children got up from their warm patches of sand and ran over to the women.

'Stop! Stop!' they begged them. Mana and Tili got in between the women to prevent them from hitting one another again.

Mala went on shouting. She blamed her son-in-law, Kaj, for taking Miwa as a second wife, and neglecting his first wife, Lilil.

'You are putting my daughter to one side!' she said.

'Wali, wali, wali!' all the kids sang out. 'Alright, alright, alright, that's enough! We want to go back to sleep now, it's cold!' They all stood there, shivering.

At last the women stopped fighting and everyone settled down.

A SAD STORY

On one occasion, Mana's family was camping at Nimpi, a jila. Mana had gone hunting with her sister, while their mother and father were away hunting somewhere else. All the smaller children were playing on the flat ground near the camp.

Yinti, Kana and two other boys took Mana's little brother, Parri, her blind mother's last son, into the sandhills to get some gum from a nyalyka tree. The boys broke off pieces of hard gum to chew and gave some to the little fellow. He put it in his mouth and tried to swallow it. The gum got stuck in his throat and he started choking, but the children had no water to give him to wash it down. His mother was sitting in the shade and couldn't see what was happening.

The boys got frightened and took the little boy back to his mother, coughing and choking. Yinti said to her, 'Sister, your little boy ate some gum.'

When the boy's mother realised that her son was choking, she started to cry. She gave him water and some milk from her breast, but he couldn't swallow properly. Some time in the afternoon, he died. The four bigger boys were frightened and they all ran away.

When Mana's mother and then her father came back to camp, they found everyone crying and learnt that the little boy was dead. Mana's father cried for his little son and hit himself on the forehead with the sharp edge of a boomerang, till blood was running down his face. All the other kids, the sisters and brothers of that little boy, were wailing too.

Mana's older sister Pali and Yinti's mother, Mala, carried the boy's body away from the camp and buried him in the sand.

Mana was sad for a long time. She had loved that little boy. He was unusual to look at, light-skinned like his father.

Mana's blind mother wouldn't be comforted. She sat down in the shade, crying, and refused to move. Mana's father and mother and other people brought back goanna meat and nuts for her and looked after her, but she didn't want to eat.

When it was time to move on, the blind woman refused to go with her family. 'No, leave me here,' she told them. Her husband wouldn't hear of it, so the other adults took turns carrying her to the next waterhole, Wirrikarijarti. She kept crying over the loss of her last child.

The family moved on to the main jila at Tapu. On the way, they left the blind woman behind. They settled her under a shady tree with some food and a coolamon of water, and went on without her.

At the time, Mana didn't know why they had left her blind mother behind.

All Mana's father would say was, 'We can't take her with us any more. We'll have to leave her here.' He cried and hit himself on the forehead with a boomerang, and Pali hit herself on the top of the head with a rock till blood ran down her face. Mana was crying too. They all had to walk away and leave her blind mother.

No one wanted to talk about it then, but later Mana learnt that her blind mother had asked to be left behind. Without her last remaining child, she had nothing left to live for.

'Take me and leave me,' she had said again and again. When he could see that she wasn't going to change her mind, her husband had finally agreed to do as she asked. He took her to a shady tree not far from the waterhole and everyone walked away in tears, leaving her to die alone.

Dying in the Desert

People who grew up in the desert claim that most people were healthy. There were no epidemics of influenza and other such diseases. However, blindness was not uncommon, perhaps caused mainly by trachoma.

When a desert person died, everyone would cry aloud. Close relations would hit themselves on the head – men with boomerangs and women with rocks – to show their grief. They would then go on a meat fast, refusing to eat red meat. Other people would bring them permissible meat such as goannas. The blind woman refused to eat anything, not because she was following the custom of fasting, but because she had no will to live.

Old and infirm people who could no longer keep travelling with the family group would sometimes ask to be left behind. 'Take me and leave me,' they would say, and relations, recognising that the end was approaching, would lead the old person away from the waterhole and leave them with just a coolamon of water and some food, knowing that, once the water ran out, the old person would die. Mana's blind mother became so depressed after losing the last of her children that she could no longer make the effort to stay alive and, like an old person, asked to be left behind.

Bitten By a Dog

Mana once had a big, black dog, which had the same name she did: Mana. He was a bad-tempered dog and people thought he was dangerous and kept away from him. Because he was said to be vicious, no one called him by his name. Mana was fond of him because he was a good hunter, as poor Blacknose had been, often bringing game for her to cook, but she was always a little wary of him.

One afternoon, when Mana was down in the waterhole, filling up a coolamon, the black dog got into the waterhole too. He jumped in and started snarling at Mana, as if he was going to bite her. She was frightened but just stood still, not moving, and waited to see what would happen. The dog didn't bite her; he just finished drinking and jumped out of the waterhole.

The black dog did bite Mana another time. It was when he had caught a minijarti — a lizard like a blue-tongue, but paler in colour — and Mana was trying to pull it away from him so that she could cook it. The dog bit her on the upper arm, then grabbed his lizard and ran away.

Afterwards, when Mana's uncle Yinti heard what had happened, he wanted to spear the dog, but Mana said, 'No, leave him alone; don't hurt this dog — he's mine. He's a good hunter, you know, he brings meat.' Yinti listened to her and the dog stayed with Mana.

DOGS

People were attached to their dogs and didn't like to see them hurt or killed. Mana valued her black dog because he was such a good hunter, even though he was unpredictable and once bit her.

A TRICK

One time in the cool season, when the weather had turned cold and rainy, Mana went to Wirtukawarnti with her sister Pali, who was now a young woman, and their granny, Jaja.

On this day, Jaja and her two granddaughters went off hunting together, taking their dogs with them. One of Jaja's dogs was sick, and she was carrying him.

After they had walked for a good while, Jaja wanted to rest. She put her dog under a tree and they all sat down. When it was time to move, Mana got up to go, but Jaja wanted her to stay there with the dog, while she went hunting with Pali.

'You stay here, girl,' Jaja told Mana. 'Keep the dog with you, he's sick. We'll catch some game and come back later.'

'No, I'm not looking after your dog,' Mana told her Jaja. 'You stay with him. He's your dog — I've got two dogs already. I want to go hunting.'

But Jaja insisted, so with bad grace Mana stayed at the dinner camp with Jaja's sick dog while the others went off to get meat for dinner, taking Mana's dogs with them. Sulkily, Mana watched them go.

The day was damp and cold; there was not much wind, but the sky was covered with grey cloud and winter rain was coming up. They needed a fire.

Mana left the ailing dog by the tree and went off some way to gather firewood. She found some wood from a dead yarun tree, the sort that burns for a long time and makes good coals. Instead of dragging wood all the way back to the dinner camp, Mana decided to make a fire right there.

She collected some dead, light grass from the base of a tree, where it wasn't too damp, and broke off some small pieces of dry bark, leaves and twigs from the underside of a dead tree trunk. Using her jarra to

set fire to the tinder grass and bark, Mana added more wood, twig by tiny twig. She blew on the flame until she had a good little fire going. She added more wood to build it up, then laid a big log on it. She sat there for a while, enjoying the heat.

Even though the weather was cold, Mana didn't stay by the fire for long, but went back to the dinner camp to wait with the dog for the others to come back.

When Jaja and Pali came back to the dinner camp with the animals they'd caught, it was late in the afternoon, close to dusk. Mana asked them, 'How are you going to cook that meat with no fire?'

'Didn't you make a fire?' asked Pali, crossly. 'What did you do with the firestick? Don't tell me you let it go out? You know you should always keep the jarra burning! How are we going to make a fire? It's too damp to start one with kungkala.'

'Rain's coming up,' said Jaja. 'I'm going to cover myself with sand and go to sleep here.'

'No, it's too cold,' said Mana. 'Let's go back to the jila.' Darkness was falling, it had started to rain and none of them really wanted to stay there overnight, with no food and no fire. There would be other people at the waterhole, and they were sure to have a fire going.

'Oh, why didn't you keep that jarra alight?' Pali asked, angrily. 'I'm tired from hunting and now we've got to walk for half the night.'

They all started walking, with Mana in front, and she led the others towards the place where she'd made the fire. In the darkness, Jaja and Pali didn't see any smoke,

FIRE

Although the desert is hot for most of the year, during a few months in the dry season temperatures can drop very low, especially at night, and strong winds make the cold worse. Very occasionally, 'winter rain' falls for a few days in the dry season, and then the cold lasts all day.

Fire was important in the desert, for cooking food and, in the cold weather, for keeping warm. People also set fire to dense spinifex to clear the land for hunting. Desert people could make fire by friction, using two pieces of a certain type of wood or kungkala. This was hard work, requiring some strength, and people avoided having to do it every time they needed to light a fire by carrying a jarra, or firestick, which they used like a taper.

In wet weather, people often covered their fire with bark and sand while they went hunting, and uncovered the embers when they came back.

but as they got close, they suddenly caught sight of red coals glowing on the sand.

'What's this?' asked Jaja, as she realised Mana had been teasing them. 'Ah, you did make a fire for us!' The old woman was happy to be able to stop and rest.

Mana started laughing, but Pali didn't think it was funny at all.

'You shouldn't tell lies,' she scolded. 'I'll hit you!' She raised her kana but didn't hit Mana; in truth, she was glad that Mana had made a fire after all.

They cooked the animals they'd caught: a possum, a yellow goanna and a black goanna. They ate some of the meat and stowed the rest in a tree for the following day. Then they scooped out their sleeping hollows in the sand and lay down close to the fire. Mana woke up once or twice in the night when she heard her grandmother stoking the fire with more wood.

Early next morning, the trio set off for Wirtukawarnti to join the rest of the family. They gave some of the meat to Yinti's father. Kaj was there with his wife, Miwa. Yinti had gone to another waterhole with his mother and younger brother Kana.

After they'd shared the meat around, Mana said to Miwa, 'Let's go to Jarriri, you, me and the two dogs.' They left the kids behind with Miwa's husband Kaj.

Mana and Miwa walked all the way to Jarriri rockhole with the two dogs. They didn't stop to sleep but just kept walking through the night till they got there. Jarriri was the conception site for Mana's little brother — the place where his parents had dreamed they were going to have a baby, before they knew his mother was carrying him.

The two women went looking for food and found a lot of tartaku and kumpupaja. Then they followed the tracks of a cat; the two dogs chased it and caught it.

The others didn't come looking for them; they left the women to themselves. The pair of them brought back some game as well as some of the kumpupaja they'd found at Jarriri.

When they got back to camp, Mana gave her mother some tartaku and kumpupaja, then they cooked the cat. Mana's mother had been in mourning, fasting from meat since the death of her blind 'sister', but it was time to come out of the fast, so Mana gave her some of the cat meat by rubbing it on her lips, and then her mother had to eat it. Mana was proud to be the one who gave her mother meat to break her fast.

Mana knew she should never let her jarra go out. She wasn't yet strong enough to make fire from scratch, using sticks. Her mother could make fire by sawing a piece of wood with another piece, or by twirling one stick on another until they were smouldering hot, but it was hard work. Everyone preferred to carry a jarra. They always made their jarra from long-burning wood, and lit one end from the campfire before they went hunting. The flame would go out, but the wood stayed smouldering. When they wanted to light another fire, they just had to blow on it to bring up the flame again.

Only once did Mana experience losing fire. She and her sister were staying at Pinturr with their granny during the hot weather. They caught game and gathered desert nuts, but their firestick went out and they couldn't cook their food. Pali tried to make a fire with two sticks she broke from a kungkala tree, but she couldn't manage it. Jaja was getting old then, and she couldn't do it any more either, so they had to go somewhere else to find fire.

They picked up their raw meat and nuts and carried it all with them. Next morning they arrived at Ngapajarra — Two Waterholes. Mana's brother and some older people were there already; they made a fire for the hungry old woman and her granddaughters, so that at last they could cook their food.

FOOD AND FASTING

Desert people ate a variety of food. Goannas, a type of large lizard, were common and not hard to catch in their burrows. There were mammals such as possums, and even cats, which had been introduced from Europe but had already colonised the desert. People also gathered various types of small fruit, such as kumpupaja, tartaku (bloodwood galls), and nuts from the Turtujarti tree.

In this story, Mana's mother is still fasting from red meat since her co-wife, or 'sister' died. To bring a mourner's fast to an end, after sometimes many months, another member of the family would rub a piece of cooked meat on that person's lips, and then he or she would be able to eat red meat again.

MANA THE HUNTER

Another time, when Kaj and his other wife had gone to camp near Paparta waterhole, Miwa went hunting. She left Mana to look after her two boys, Riji and Karli. Mana had two dogs there as well, Kiji, who had a lot of puppies, and Kiji's mate, Malji.

'You stay here and look after the two little boys,' Miwa told Mana.

Mana stayed behind with the boys because she had to, but she really wanted to go hunting. After a while, she said to the two boys:

'You two stay here in the shade with the puppies. I'll go and catch some lizards for us to eat.'

'No, don't leave us!' Karli wailed. 'Someone might come along and kill us!'

'A bad spirit might get us!' said Riji.

'No, you'll be all right,' said Mana. 'I won't go far and I'll bring back something good for a snack.'

Mana went off on her own, not too far from camp, and killed some small lizards. She noticed the fresh track of a cat and wanted to follow it, but she couldn't leave the boys behind so she just took the lizards back to camp. She used her firestick to make a fire and cooked the lizards.

'You want some meat?' she asked the boys. Then she shared it out. The three of them ate the lizards, giving the skin and bones to the puppies to chew on.

Not long afterwards, Miwa came back with two goannas and a coolamon full of wattle seeds.

'Good,' thought Mana. 'She can look after her boys now.'

'I'm going hunting now,' she told Miwa. 'I saw the tracks of a cat and I'm going to see if I can catch it. The tracks are from this morning; it would be a pity to leave it.'

'Yes, you go and catch it,' said Miwa, as she started building up the fire again to cook her game.

Mana left Miwa with the boys and took her two dogs, leaving the puppies behind. She and the dogs started following the cat. It was well ahead of them and Mana walked for a long way, while the dogs ran around sniffing.

After a while, they came to a place where the cat had been lying down resting.

'It can't be far now,' thought Mana. Sure enough, a bit further on the dogs picked up a fresh scent, and Mana could see from the tracks that the cat had started to run. The dogs raced on ahead, while Mana followed at a fast pace. Suddenly, she heard a scuffle, the cat snarling and fighting.

Soon, there was a commotion and she knew that the dogs had caught the cat. Before she had reached them, the dogs came back to her, Kiji carrying the dead cat in her jaws. Her ears were bloody from the cat's claws.

Mana carried the cat to the nearest tree and sat down, the dogs panting beside her. By now it was quite late in the afternoon. After a short rest, she gutted the cat. Then she stood up, draped the cat over her shoulders and set off walking back to camp.

It was just getting dark when Karli saw Mana coming along through the gloom.

'Mummy!' he said to Miwa. 'My sister's coming back with a cat!'

He ran along the sandhill to meet her and took the cat from her, then carried it back to camp, running ahead.

'So you got the cat; that's good,' Miwa said when Mana sat down.

Miwa had cooked her goanna, and she shared the last of it with Mana. The boys went to get more wood to build up the fire again. Miwa singed the cat's fur in the flames, then waited for the fire to burn down. She put the cat in the hot coals and covered it up with sand.

Everyone was tired now, so they left the cat to cook overnight and lay down and went to sleep.

In the morning, Mana pulled the cat out of the ashes, dusted it off and shared it out for everyone to eat. When they'd finished, they decided to head east to Tapu, the main jila in Mana's country. On the way, they noticed smoke rising from the south.

'Look, my husband's at Walypa,' said Miwa. 'They must be on their way back from Paparta.'

Miwa lit a fire in the spinifex to show the rest of the family where they were.

They went on to Tapu and waited there, and the others arrived later in the day. Kaj was carrying a dingo he'd speared, so they cooked that and everyone had a good feed.

The family all stayed at Tapu for a while, and Mana's puppies got bigger.

By now, Mana had become a good hunter. She could get cats and goannas and snakes on her own. She often went hunting with Miwa and they'd be away all day, never coming back empty-handed. Mana knew she was a better hunter than Miwa.

HUNTING

Children who were just learning to hunt could catch small lizards and cook them. However, Mana had moved on to catching goannas and cats. Cats are hard to catch. Their tracks are easy to find and follow, but a cat can run for a long time, keeping ahead of the hunter. For this reason, dogs are a great help; they can pick up a scent and run faster than the cat. They either run it to ground and kill it, or chase it up a tree and keep it there till the hunter comes along with his or her hunting stick.

COOKING

Most game is cooked in the same way: the scales of reptiles or the fur of mammals are singed off first in the flames of the fire, and when the fire has settled down the hunter rakes some glowing coals into a shallow scrape in the sand, lays the animal on top, spreads more coals over the animal and then covers the whole lot with earth or sand to keep the heat in while the meat cooks.

MANA LOSES HER FATHER

Mana's father was a big man, strong and solidly built. He was a good-natured husband and father, and never hit his wife or any of his children.

One day, during the hot weather, the whole family set off to move to a new waterhole, Kayalajarti. On the journey, Mana's father started to feel weak and had to stop and rest. They had drunk all their water, so Mana's mother told Tili and her younger brother to stay with their father while she went ahead to Kayalajarti with Pali and Mana, to fetch water in the coolamon.

It was still a long way to the jila and Mana's mother was worried about her husband, so they walked as fast as they could in the heat. When they reached the waterhole, they had to dig out the sand that had fallen in since the last time someone had been there to drink.

They filled up their coolamon with water, had a long drink themselves, and started back to find Mana's father. They took turns carrying the water.

When they got close, they heard Tili and her brother crying. As soon as their mother saw her children's faces,

she knew that she had lost her husband. While his wife and older daughters had been away, fetching water, the children's father had died.

Mana's mother put down her coolamon and started crying aloud. Pali and Mana were crying too. Then their mother picked up a rock and struck herself on the head with it, until blood was pouring down her face. Pali took the rock away from her mother to stop her from hurting herself.

There was no one to bury the dead man, so they had to leave his body there on the sand. They all went away, crying.

DEATH AND BURIAL

Like life itself, death took place in the sandhills and when someone fell seriously ill, there was often little to be done. It is possible that Mana's father was suffering from dehydration and heat stroke, and the family had no water to give him to drink or to cool him down.

Only people in a certain relationship to someone who had died would bury that person. A spouse or offspring was too closely related and would be too sad.

MANA NEARLY DIES OF THIRST

Once, Mana nearly died. She and her family and Yinti's family were camping at Kumpujarti, and in the morning Mana told Yinti's mother and father, whom she called Grandmother and Grandfather, that she was going hunting, and set off with her dogs, Kiji and Malji. She carried her long digging stick but no water; she didn't want to carry a heavy coolamon, so instead, she had a long drink of water before she set off.

Mana walked for a long way. There were not many fresh tracks on the sandhills but soon she came to a blue-tongue's burrow in the sand, with tracks going into it and none coming out. Mana knelt down and dug out the burrow with her hands. She pulled out two desert blue-tongue lizards, one after the other, and killed them. Then she tucked them through her hair-belt, one on each side, and kept walking. The lizards were for her grandparents, who were still fasting from red meat, following the death of Mana's father. After another good while, she noticed the fresh tracks of a wallaby. She started to follow them, at the same time calling her dogs.

'Yii, yii, yii, yii!' she said, urging them on.

Kiji and Malji quickly picked up the scent of the animal and went racing after it. Mana followed, walking fast. She soon lost sight of her dogs, but she could see what was happening by watching their tracks. The wallaby was running now and the dogs were right behind.

Then Mana heard the dogs yelping and snarling.

'Ah, they've got it!' Mana said to herself and broke into a run. She saw a scuffle in the spinifex some way ahead. By the time she'd caught up with the dogs they had nearly done for the wallaby. Mana pulled the animal away, threw it on the ground and killed it with a few quick blows of her digging stick. By now, Mana was hot and tired, so she carried the wallaby to the nearest tree and sat down in the shade. She felt the wallaby's soft, furry belly; it was nice and fat. She would gut the animal later. Kiji and Malji flopped down beside her, panting hard.

Mana lay down in the shade and dozed off. After a while, she woke up, feeling thick-headed; she needed a drink. She sat there a little longer, then got up and started heading back towards camp. Kiji and Malji followed.

The journey seemed much longer going home than it had coming out in the morning. Mana was tired now, and she was carrying a whole wallaby, which seemed to become heavier as she went on. Every once in a while, she stopped to rest with the dogs under a tree. They were all really thirsty.

At long last, Mana was in sight of the family camp at Kumpujarti. She staggered over the last sandhill towards the water. Kiji and Malji ran ahead, jumped into the waterhole and drank thirstily. Mana came along behind and dropped the wallaby under a tree. Just as she reached the waterhole, her legs gave way. She managed to crawl up to the water, where she leaned her head over and drank. She tried to get up then, but her body collapsed, and she rolled onto her back, unconscious.

It was Law time, and a young boy was sitting in a special Law camp, some distance away from the main camp. He suddenly got a feeling that something was wrong. Because he was going through Law, he wasn't allowed to speak, but he took up his hunting stick and beat it against the ground to attract attention. An old man went to him. He understood from hand signs what the boy was trying to tell him, and hurried up to the camp at Kumpujarti, where he found Mana's grandfather.

'Where's that girl?' the old man asked. 'Something might be wrong.'

'She went hunting this morning,' said her grandfather, 'but she should have come back by now.'

'I'll go and look for her,' said Mana's grandmother, and hurried down to the waterhole. As she drew near, she could see Mana lying motionless on the ground. Jaja started to cry. When she came close, she knelt down and put her hand on Mana's head. It was hot and clammy. She could see that Mana was still breathing, so she picked her up and carried the unconscious girl on her back to the camp and laid her down in the shade. Taking mouthfuls of water, Jaja pursed her lips and sprayed it over Mana's body. Gradually, Mana began to cool down and soon she opened her eyes. Jaja gave her water to sip. When she was feeling a bit stronger, Mana sat up and drank more water, little by little.

'I thought I was going to die,' she said later.

Jaja went back for the wallaby and brought it up to camp. She opened its belly with a stone knife and pulled out the guts, throwing them to the dogs. Then she dug a pit near the cooking fire and laid the wallaby in the coals to cook. She put in the two blue-tongue lizards as well. That night, all the people and their dogs had a good feed.

INTUITION

In this story we are reminded of the scarcity of water in the desert as well as the intense heat. We learn of a young lad who is going through his initiation. Obliged to stay in one place and not allowed to speak, he is perhaps more sensitive to what goes on around him, and his intuition tells him that Mana is in distress.

PAKART

Mana's dog Kiji was a tame female dingo and a good hunter. Mana and her family used to take her hunting for cats and sandhill goannas. Kiji and her mate, Malji, had several litters of puppies.

One sad day, when they were out hunting, Kiji, who had not long ago given birth to puppies, was bitten by a venomous snake. Mana and her sister followed her tracks and found her dead.

Without their mother to feed them, the puppies started to die, but Mana wanted to save one of them. She chose a fluffy little male puppy to keep, but it needed milk.

Kaj and his two wives, Lilil and Miwa, had recently come back from the station to visit their relations. Miwa was still feeding Karli and had milk in her breasts, so she fed the puppy as well as her little boy. Karli and his older brother Riji grew up with that puppy and called him 'brother', because he had shared their mother's milk. That meant he was Mana's 'brother' too.

When they came back from the station, Kaj and his wives and all the kids were wearing clothes, and they brought presents for their relations. One of the things they brought was some soda soap. People on the stations made their own soap from bullock fat and soda.

Kaj showed everyone the soap as a novelty and gave some to Mana's granny, but she didn't use it. She just put it to one side, and buried it in the sand under a tree. The desert people had no use for soap. They just used water for drinking, and cleaned themselves with sand.

One day, when that little woolly puppy was getting bigger and playing around, he found the soap and dug it up. The bullock fat must have smelt good to him, so he ate it. The soap made him sick; he was frothing at the mouth and jumping around. Then he started staggering and fell down, as if he was going to die.

'What's wrong with my brother?' said Mana. 'Look, he's been eating that soap; maybe it's poison!'

Jaja picked up the puppy and gave him water to drink, then massaged his stomach to make him vomit. After he had brought up all the soap, the puppy began to get better.

When a baby is just learning to walk, it staggers and falls down on the sand, then tries again and keeps falling down. A baby that reaches that stage is called 'pakartparta'. After the puppy had eaten the soap he was staggering around like that and falling down, so people called him Pakart — Staggers.

Pakart grew up to be a big dog, like a wild dingo, and really fierce. Once, he stole a piece of meat from Mana's hand. She tried to get it back from him and he bit her, right in the soft part of her arm. Blood was pouring and Mana went to show her parents, who were over near the waterhole, and they tied up her arm with strips of bark. All the same, she did get her meat back.

Much later, when Kaj and his family were leaving the desert again, they took Pakart with them to Cherrabun Station. At Timber Creek, where some of their relations were looking after the bore, Pakart ate poisoned bait, which had been put out for wild dingoes. He ran around in agony, then fell down, dead.

Mana didn't know what had happened to Pakart until much later, when her turn came to leave the desert and stay at Timber Creek.

MANA GETS MARRIED

Times were changing for desert people. More and more of them were drifting to the sheep and cattle stations to the north. Pali left with her promised husband and never came back. Fewer and fewer people were still living in the sandhills.

One year, when Kaj returned to Cherrabun with his growing family, Yinti went too. He came back a year later with stories of such a different world that Mana and Tili were entranced.

Mana was growing up. Her body had become that of a young woman, and it was time for her to be given to her husband. Both she and her young sister, Tili, had been promised to the same man, whose name was Kurru. His main waterhole was Japingka, the same as Yinti's, and the girls already knew him.

One day in the cold-weather time, when Kurru was camping nearby, Jaja told Mana to take some seed bread to Kurru. He accepted the gift and in return he gave some meat to Mana to take back to her parents, his mother- and father-in-law. After that, Mana went to live in her husband's camp. Tili came with her, to get to know the man she too was expected to marry one day.

Kurru had left the sandhill country once, with Yinti, and spent time on Cherrabun cattle station. He had returned to the desert, but he knew that most people were leaving, going one way, never coming back. He knew that, sooner or later, he too would take his new wife to live on the station. Meanwhile, desert life went on as usual for the dwindling number of people.

The young couple moved to another waterhole. One day, a huge animal came to the water to drink. Mana had never seen anything like it; it was big and brown, with white markings on its face, and it had what looked like sharp branches or sticks coming out of its head.

'Look, look — a bullock!' said Kurru. 'I'm going to kill it.'

Mana tried to stop him. 'No, no!' she said. 'Don't spear

it; I'm frightened! It might get angry and attack you with those things on its head!'

'It's for meat, that one,' said Kurru. He went down into the flat, downwind of the bullock, and then crept up as close to it as he could before he let fly with his spear.

The spear hit the bullock in the ribs and went right through its body, the point coming out on the other side. The bullock crumpled and lay down, making a strange noise: 'Moo, moo.' Then Kurru hooked another spear into his spear-thrower and pierced him again. The second blow was lethal, and the bullock kicked and lay still.

After that, Kurru and Mana cut pieces of meat from the bullock's body and put them in the fire to cook. When the meat was done, Kurru pulled it out and gave some to his wife. This was the first time Mana had eaten beef. The rest of the cooked meat the couple carried to Purturnjarti, where their families were camping, and shared it with everyone. The children were excited about trying the new meat, and said they liked it.

MARRIAGE

There was no special ceremony to celebrate marriage in the desert. When a girl had reached puberty and was considered mature enough to marry, there would be an exchange of gifts of food, and she then went to live with her promised husband. A younger wife might join her husband's family group even earlier, to get to know his older wife or wives and become familiar with his country before she took on the full responsibilities of marriage. Sons-in-law had an obligation to help provide for their wives' parents.

Not long after this, the whole family group moved to Kunajarti and stayed there for a while. Kurru started talking about going to live on Cherrabun Station. He told Mana what it was like there: so much food and meat that no one had to go hunting, and all sorts of new things, like cars and windmills. Mana knew that many of her relations were living on the station already. Yinti had gone back, this time taking his mother and Kana with him. And so, still with some misgivings, she agreed to go.

When the couple told their families of their plans, the old people were sad. Kurru wanted to take everyone with him, but his grandparents and Mana's Jaja said they were too old to travel so far. They told Kurru they would stay behind in their own country. Mana's mother said she would stay with her own mother, Mana's Jaja, who, with her bad back, would need someone to look after her. Then Tili said she didn't want to go to the station either. She would stay with her mother and Jaja and her little brother.

When the dry season was over and the rains were just starting, and they knew that the waterholes would be filling up again, Mana and Kurru set off with Kurru's mother and father and his younger sister. Everyone else stayed behind. It would be thirty years before Mana saw her country again.

WALMAJARRI PRONUNCIATION GUIDE

Like most Australian languages, Walmajarri uses some sounds that do not occur in English. Because of the limitations of the English (Roman) alphabet, these sounds are in most cases expressed by a combination of two letters, eg the consonants 'ng', 'ny', 'rl', 'rt'.

There are also some English sounds, such as those written 'f', 'h', 's', 'e' and 'o', which are not found in Walmajarri.

In Kimberley languages, no distinction is made between the sounds in the pairs written in English as 'b' and 'p', 'd' and 't', 'g' and 'k'. For this reason, only one of each pair of letters is used in the written languages. Some languages, including Walmajarri, use 'p', 't' and 'k'. Others use 'b', 'd' and 'g' instead, but the choice is arbitrary.

a	like u in but
aa	long a as in pa or ah
i	like i in big
iyi	like ee in greet
j	like j in just
k	like g in girl or k in kill
l	like l in lamp
ly	like lli in million
m	like m in mother
n	like n in nut
ng	like ng in singer
ny	like ni in onion
p	like b in boy or p in pal
r	like r in parade
rl	like American pronunciation of rl in curl; r is sounded
rn	like American pronunciation of rn in corn; r is sounded
rr	rolled r as in Scottish and Italian r
rt	like American pronunciation of rt in party; r is sounded
t	like d in drum or t in tap
u	like u in pull; not like u in but
uwu	long u as in clue
w	like w in window
y	like y in yellow. Note: y at the end of a word modifies the preceding letter (n or l). It is never an extra syllable as in many.

WALMAJARRI GLOSSARY

Japi	a landscape feature near a jila where the resident jila snake comes up from underground to look out. The japi might be a rock, a sandhill formation or a small hill
Jaja	mother's mother; woman's daughter's child (a reciprocal term)
Japingka	an important jila, where people used to gather in the hot time of year and perform ceremonies
Jarra	firestick, which people carried around to light fires
Jarriny	conception place and totem
Jila	'living water'; waterhole that never runs dry and home of a spirit snake
Jumu	temporary waterhole, which holds water for a time after rain but eventually runs dry
Jurnta	a small, edible bulb of a desert grass that grows in salty ground

Kana	digging stick, used mainly by women
Kartiya	non-Aboriginal person, especially of European descent. Term used across the Kimberley
Kayalajarti	name of a waterhole
Kukurr	a mischievous spirit
Kumpupaja	greenish fruit of small shrub, Solanum sp.
Kunajarti	name of a waterhole
Kungkala	type of wood used to make fire by friction; the short sticks used for this purpose
Kurra	stone axe; the sharpened axe heads were attached to wooden handles with animal sinews and spinifex wax
Lantimangu	place name of a particular japi, Mana's conception site
Mana	tree
Mantarta	name of a jila
Minijarti	Great Desert Skink (Egernia kintorei), a burrowing lizard with a pale skin, once common, now an endangered species
Ngapajarra	name of a double waterhole
Ngawiji	grandmother (father's mother)
Nimpi	name of a jila
Nyalyka	type of tree
Pakartparta	toddler
Paparta	name of a waterhole
Pinturr	name of a waterhole
Purturnjarti	name of a waterhole

Puyurruyurru	edible insect
Tapu	the main jila in Mana's country
Tartaku	edible bloodwood gall made by insects
Turtujarti	Desert Walnut Tree (Owenia reticulata); produces abundant nuts and an edible gum
Wali	All right; that's it, then; an expression used to bring a conversation or discussion to a close
Walypa	name of a waterhole
Warawu!	an exclamation of alarm or dismay
Wirrikarijarti	name of a waterhole
Wirtuka	plant that grows along the ground near a waterhole; has edible roots
Wirtukawarnti	name of a waterhole
Wurruwurru	spirit baby
Yakapiri	Bird-flower Bush (Crotalaria cunninghamii); a shrub that grows on sandhills
Yarun	type of tree (Corymbia aff. Chippendalei)
Yii!	call to a dog, urging it on in a hunt

ABOUT THE CREATORS

Jukuna Mona Chuguna

Jukuna Mona Chuguna was a Walmajarri woman from the Great Sandy Desert in Western Australia, where she grew up. As a young bride she left the desert with her husband in the 1950s, to live and work on cattle and sheep stations in the Kimberley's Fitzroy Valley. From the late 1960s, Jukuna worked with linguists who were studying Walmajarri. She taught them her language and at the same time learnt to read and write it herself. In middle age, Jukuna took up painting and became a well-regarded artist, holding exhibitions of her work around Australia and overseas. She was a natural teacher and great storyteller. She died in 2011.

Pat Lowe

Pat Lowe hails from England and, after doing some globetrotting, fulfilled her childhood ambition to settle in Western Australia. She spent a few years in Perth, working as a psychologist in child welfare and in prisons. She then applied for transfer to the Regional Prison in Broome, where she moved in 1979. In 1986, Pat went to live in a desert camp with Jukuna's uncle and age-mate, Jimmy Pike, where she came to know Jukuna and her family. Later in life, when both Pat and Jukuna were living in Broome, they worked together to record Jukuna's stories.

Mervyn Street

Mervyn Street is a Gooniyandi artist, who was born on Louisa Downs Station in the Kimberley region of Western Australia. In his youth he worked as a stockman and later developed his artistic talents. Mervyn has produced many paintings, drawings and prints of station life. Nowadays, Mervyn has his own community at Pullout Springs, and divides his time between drawing and painting at Mangkaja Arts in Fitzroy Crossing and teaching the Gooniyandi language at the Yiyili Community school.

FURTHER READING

Pat Lowe, illustrated by Jimmy Pike, *Yinti Desert Child*, Magabala Books, Broome, 1992

Pat Lowe, illustrated by Jimmy Pike, *Desert Dog*, Magabala Books, Broome,1997

Pat Lowe & Jimmy Pike, *You Call it Desert — We Used to Live There*, Magabala Books, Broome, second edition 2009

Eirlys Richards, Joyce Hudson, Pat Lowe (Eds.) *Out of the Desert — Stories from the Walmajarri Exodus*, Magabala Books, 2002

Ngarta Jinny Bent, Jukuna Mona Chuguna, Pat Lowe & Eirlys Richards, *Two Sisters Ngarta and Jukuna*, Fremantle Press, 2004

Pat Lowe, *In the Desert — Jimmy Pike as a Boy*, Penguin Books, 2007

Jimmy Pike, *The Art of Fire*, Backroom Press, Broome, 2008

Joyce Hudson & Eirlys Richards, *The Walmajarri Dictionary*, Summer Institute of Linguistics, Darwin, 1990, second edition 2012. Digital version at: www.ausil.org.au

Some of these books are now out of print but may be obtained through libraries or purchased second-hand.

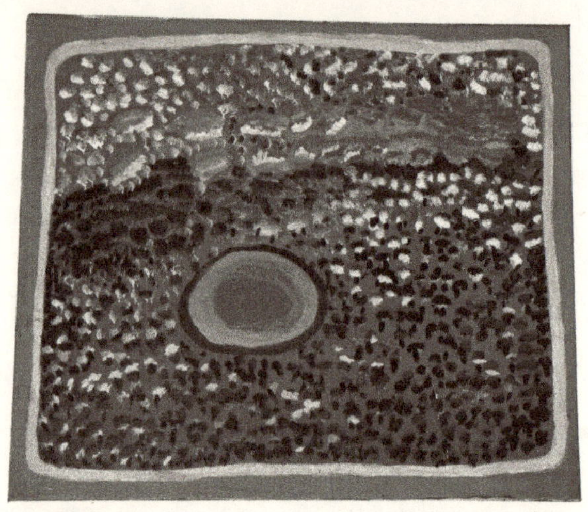

NGAPA PUKURNPUKURN

FLOWERS NEAR WATER

Jukuna Mona Chuguna

When it rains the rockholes overflow. The wet ground around the rockholes sets the grass seeds growing and later the flowers are everywhere. We call this sight ngapa pukurnpukurn.

Design elements from this painting have been used in the cultural information boxes.